D0012291

HIGH SCHOOL MUSICAL 3 SENIOR YEAR

The Junior Novel
Adapted by N. B. Grace

Based on the screenplay written by Peter Barsocchini
Based on characters created by Peter Barsocchini
Executive Producer Kenny Ortega
Produced by Bill Borden and Barry Rosenbush
Directed by Kenny Ortega

DISNEP PRESS
New York

Copyright © 2008 Disney Enterprises, Inc.

All rights reserved. Published by Disney Press, an imprint of Disney Book
Group. No part of this book may be reproduced or transmitted in any form
or by any means, electronic or mechanical, including
photocopying, recording, or by any information storage and retrieval
system, without written permission from the publisher. For information
address Disney Press, 114 Fifth Avenue, New York, New York 10011-5690.

Printed in the United States of America

First Edition
1 3 5 7 9 10 8 6 4 2

Library of Congress Catalog Card Number: 2008904376

ISBN 978-1-4231-1202-0
For more Disney Press fun, visit www.disneybooks.com
Visit DisneyChannel.com

If you purchased this book without a cover, you should be aware
that this book is stolen property. It was reported as "unsold and
destroyed" to the publisher, and neither the author nor the
publisher has received any payment for this "stripped" book.

CHAPTER ONE

The East High gym was rocking as the first half of the grudge match between the East High Wildcats and the West High Knights was coming to a close. The cheerleaders for both basketball teams were leading the audience in cheers, and the East High band's drummers were pounding out a beat. But on the court, the players didn't pay attention to any sounds except their own breathing and occasional grunting as they blocked shots, jumped for rebounds, and raced across the floor.

In the middle of all the chaos, Wildcats captain Troy Bolton took a deep breath, pushed his hair out of his eyes, and glanced at the scoreboard.

The score was twenty-four for the Wildcats . . . and thirty-seven for the Knights.

Suddenly, the buzzer rang.

The first half of the game was over.

And the Wildcats were getting crushed.

As the team members piled into the locker room, their faces looked shell-shocked. Several players took a seat on the benches. They slumped over, exhausted. Others leaned on their lockers, trying not to look discouraged.

Every player's eyes turned to look at Troy. He was sitting near his best friend, the team's co-captain, Chad Danforth. Two other seniors, Zeke Baylor and Jason Cross, stood a few feet away. Troy seemed unaware of the others' anxiety. His piercing blue eyes were completely focused on the dry-erase board that had been set up at the end of the locker room.

Coach Bolton, who was Troy's father, looked

around the room. He knew how his team was feeling. And he knew he had to get them back on track. He was confident that they could come from behind in the second half. He reached out with an eraser and wiped the play diagrams off the board.

The coach looked at his teammates intently. "We've dug ourselves a hole, and the only way out is on each other's shoulders," he said firmly.

Coach Bolton continued. "No more X's and O's," he told the team. "Forget the scoreboard. Here's the number that means something. . . ." He reached out and scribbled "16" on the board. "Sixteen minutes left in the game . . . the season . . . and for the seniors on this squad . . ." He glanced over at Troy, Chad, Zeke, and Jason. ". . . sixteen minutes left in a Wildcats uniform."

He gave Troy and Chad a serious look. "Captains?"

Troy stood up. This was the moment when he had to rally the Wildcats and raise their spirits.

Fortunately, he wasn't alone. "Hey, you heard Coach. The sixteen minutes are going to stay with us for a long time after we leave East High . . . so it's now or never," he said. "Chad?" he asked, glancing over at his co-captain.

As Troy expected, Chad jumped up and stood next to him. He looked over at the other Wildcats and smiled.

"What team?" he cheered enthusiastically.

The players grinned. They could always count on Troy and Chad to raise their spirits. "Wildcats!" they yelled back in unison.

"What team?" Chad shouted even louder.

"WILDCATS!" This time, their shouts rattled the roof.

Chad stepped forward and held out his right hand. Once more, he cried out, "What team?"

Nine hands joined his in the middle of a circle. "Wildcats!" everyone cheered.

Their hands flew into the air, and then the teammates burst out of the locker room into the Hallway of Champions and headed back to the gym. After Troy's pep talk and Chad's rousing cheer, they were totally fired up.

Maybe, Troy thought, a little *too* fired up . . .

He stopped at the door to the gym and turned to face his teammates. "Yo, one other thing—"

Everyone turned to look at him.

"Did anyone actually *wash* their lucky socks?" Troy asked, giving them all a serious stare. "The same socks we've worn for three straight playoff games . . . games we *won*?"

Small smiles appeared on everyone's faces as soon as they realized what Troy's question was leading up to.

"Mine never left my locker all season," Chad said proudly.

"I kept mine in my lunch bag," Jason added.

Troy nodded, satisfied. "Zeke?"

"I vacuum-packed mine," Zeke said with a laugh.

Troy grinned. "That's what I'm talking about!"

The tension eased as everyone burst out

laughing. Now we're ready to play, Troy thought with satisfaction as he threw open the doors, and the team ran back out to center court.

The Wildcats knew one thing as the second half of the game started—like Troy said, it was now or never. If they wanted to win, they had to go full throttle. And from the moment they hit the floor, that's what they did.

Troy was everywhere, motioning for his teammates to follow the plays they'd practiced for months. Chad passed the ball and ran toward the net, ready to dunk a basket for two points.

The game raged on, and the Wildcats kept piling up points. Coach Bolton paced intensely on the sidelines, matched step for step by the West High coach, who was walking up and down the sidelines on the other side of the court. The East High cheerleaders, led by Martha Cox, pulled out their best cheers to pump up the team.

In the bleachers, Gabriella Montez was

watching anxiously. The Wildcats were catching up, but time was ticking away. Would they actually be able to pull off a victory?

As the scoreboard counted off the seconds, the action got even more heated, and Troy was knocked to the ground, causing the referee to call a foul against West High. Stunned, Troy looked around the gym at the crowd yelling, the cheerleaders leaping into the air . . . and then he found Gabriella in the sea of faces. Her eyes met his and, just like that, he was back in the game.

He stepped up to the line and sank two free throws with ease.

The crowd erupted in cheers. It was anyone's game now.

On the sidelines, Coach Bolton rapidly sketched a play. The team ran over and the coach told them what they needed to do.

Troy nodded toward the end of the bench, where Jimmie "the Rocket" Zara was sitting.

Jimmie's friend, Donny Dion, was sitting next to him. They were both sophomores new to the team, and a little in awe of being in a championship game.

The coach smiled to himself. He and Troy had had exactly the same thought.

"Jimmie Z, you're in!" Coach Bolton yelled.

The other Wildcats exchanged shocked glances, but no one was more surprised than Jimmie. He was so surprised, in fact, that he ripped off his warm-up jacket too fast and ended up removing his jersey as well. As the crowd around him chuckled, the coach gathered his team into a huddle.

Across the court, the West High Knights were staring at the Wildcats with determination. They wanted the championship trophy as badly as the Wildcats did.

But Troy didn't even notice. He was too focused on what he had to do. Next to him, Jimmie was bouncing on his toes, filled with energy and trying to settle his nerves.

"Save it for the game, Rocketman," Troy said. "And keep your eyes on me."

And then they were back in the action for the last play. . . .

As the ref blew his whistle, the Wildcats all leaned down to touch their lucky socks. Then they were on the court, running the decoy play they had practiced so many times.

Chad threw the ball in bounds to Zeke, who fired it right back at Chad. Troy was surrounded by three players for the Knights, but he managed to slip free and grab a shovel pass from Chad. He set up for a jump shot and every person in the gym looked at the basket . . . except for Troy.

Instead of taking the shot, he passed the ball to Jimmie, who was completely unguarded. Jimmie hesitated for a split-second, then made a layup for two points just as the buzzer sounded.

The fake had worked!

The Wildcats had won!

Fans poured onto the gym floor, cheering

and giving each other high fives. The Wildcats mascot joined them and pulled off the head to his costume. It was none other than Ryan Evans, grinning broadly as he joined in the celebration.

Troy's teammates lifted him onto their shoulders, and the championship trophy was passed up to him.

Once again, his eyes found Gabriella's in the crowd, and he grinned. Then he lifted the trophy high in the air in celebration.

Troy's and Chad's mothers were putting the last touches on a spread of food when the two boys burst into the Boltons' kitchen. Chad grabbed his mom and gave her an exuberant hug.

"So . . . what'd you think of the game?" he asked, smiling.

She gave him a loving squeeze back. "Did you have to take it down to the buzzer? I was a nervous wreck!" she exclaimed.

Troy spun his own mother around before hugging her also.

"Back-to-back championships!" he yelled. Last year, he didn't think anything could top the feeling of the Wildcats winning the district championship. *Now*, of course, there was something better—winning two in a row!

"Fantastic!" his mom exclaimed. She put on a mock motherly voice. "But you're still helping us clean up after the party."

Troy and Chad glanced over at Zeke, who was also in the kitchen. He was still wearing his Wildcats uniform but had added a chef's hat and an apron. He was carefully putting icing on an array of basketball-shaped cupcakes.

As Chad reached out to snag one, Zeke playfully slapped his hand away. "They're cooling. I'll let you know when they're ready!" Zeke exclaimed, laughing. "Out of my kitchen, mister!"

As more Wildcats made their way from the game to the Boltons' house, the party began picking up steam. Troy maneuvered his way in between a barbecue grill, a spirited game of Ping-Pong, and groups of kids dancing, his eyes searching for Gabriella.

Finally, there was a break in the crowd and he found her. He gave Gabriella a broad smile and reached for her hand. "Hey! Fix you a plate?" he offered.

Gabriella inhaled and smelled the spicy, mouthwatering barbecue, heard the sizzle of hamburgers on the grill, and eyed the spread of side dishes being laid out. "One of everything," she said with a grin.

But just then, Chad, Troy's dad, and Coach Kellog, the University of Albuquerque basketball coach, walked over to them. Gabriella politely stepped aside.

Coach Bolton was beaming with pride. "Coach Kellog, you got any empty lockers up at U of A?"

The college coach looked over at Troy and Chad. "Not for long, I hope," he said with a smile.

Just then, Chad's father walked up to them.

Coach Bolton threw an arm around his shoulder and motioned to Coach Kellog.

"I bet Charlie Danforth will suit up for you next season, too, if you just ask him," Troy's dad joked.

Mr. Danforth grinned. "A front-row seat will do just fine," he said.

"Well, the kind of team play I saw tonight goes a long way with me," Coach Kellog commented.

Troy and Chad exchanged high fives while their dads looked on proudly.

Coach Kellog gave Troy and Chad an inquisitive look. "And we're counting on seeing you both in Redhawk uniforms next season, right?"

"Done deal," Chad replied, nodding his head.

"Amen to that, son!" Chad's father cheered.

Troy smiled weakly, then excused himself as soon as he could. He wandered around the backyard and craned his neck, searching for Gabriella again. He spotted her on the other side of the yard and started heading in her direction, but only managed to take a few steps before being intercepted by Jimmie Zara, whose face was beaming with excitement.

"Dude, great house!" Jimmie shouted. "Your room is *way* cool."

Troy raised his eyebrows. "You were in my room?"

Jimmie nodded proudly. "I took a picture. Look." He held up his digital camera so Troy could see the tiny screen.

As Troy looked at the photo of his bedroom, Jimmie added, "I'm doing mine the same way."

"Wow," Troy commented, unsure about how to react. *Or* about how to escape. "That's great, Jimmie."

Just then, Troy had an idea. "Oh, man, I left the championship trophy in my truck . . . I hope it's still there. . . .

"Don't worry, I'm on it!" Jimmie exclaimed. He quickly headed in the direction of Troy's truck.

Troy shook his head. Then he started to look for Gabriella, *again.*

Gabriella was leaning against a tree, gazing up at the stars. She loved her friends, she loved parties, she loved celebrating a Wildcats win . . . but sometimes she just needed some time to herself.

She sighed happily. It was such a beautiful night. The only thing that would make it better was—

Suddenly, a hand grabbed her arm and pulled her behind the tree.

Gabriella found herself staring up into Troy's blue eyes. He smiled down at her and motioned toward the two plates of food he had brought over. "One of everything," he said. "Your wish is my command. Now follow me."

He headed across the lawn, trying to keep both plates steady. Gabriella followed, grinning as she saw him nearly drop a plate, then recover with the grace of a champion basketball player. A few minutes later, she found herself perched high above the party in a tree house. Troy was sitting next to her with their picnic spread out before them.

"Another top secret hiding place?" Gabriella asked in a teasing voice.

"You are the second girl ever allowed up here," Troy said solemnly.

Gabriella raised one eyebrow at his comment.

He grinned. "The other was my mom, and she only climbed up to get me down. I haven't been up here since I was ten. . . ."

His voice trailed off. Gabriella gave him a questioning look.

He smiled and confessed, "Okay . . . thirteen."

She continued looking at him.

"All right," he admitted, "last week. When I was nervous about the game."

Gabriella smiled. "Well, I'm honored," she replied. "*And* ready for these . . ." she said, motioning to a plate of cupcakes. They each grabbed one.

"Was that the coach from U of A down there?" Gabriella asked, turning serious.

Troy nodded.

"I bet he's already got your name on a locker," she commented.

Troy's smile waned a bit. They both looked down at the party that was still in full swing below them. Gabriella's mother had now arrived and was chatting with Troy's parents. Troy sighed as he watched his dad's face, which was lit up with happiness over the Wildcats' win—and, Troy knew, his son's future.

Troy sighed. "Yeah, it's always been my dad's dream that I end up at his alma mater," he said.

Gabriella nodded. "My mom and I have been talking about Stanford University ever since I was born," she said.

"And you're already accepted," Troy said, trying to sound encouraging. "That's so cool."

"Except my mom *won't* stop talking about it," she admitted. "It's embarrassing."

"She's proud of you," Troy said. He paused, then added, "So am I. Everyone is."

Gabriella looked down. It was nice that everyone was proud of her, but . . .

She looked at Troy seriously. "The thing about Stanford is that it's a thousand and . . ."

Together, they both said, "Fifty-three miles—"

"From here," Troy finished the sentence. "I know. And now the rest of the school year is coming at us so fast."

There was a moment's silence. Then Gabriella said, "I wish it would all just . . . stop. At least, slow down."

Troy knew what she meant. Here they were, just months away from leaving home for the first time and being on their own . . . it was exciting. But kind of scary. Troy knew the time that they had together before the summer was over was incredibly important. He could see by the look in Gabriella's eyes that she felt the same way.

Suddenly, they were interrupted by a loud

voice. "Troy, you have guests!" Mrs. Bolton's voice called out.

She peered more closely at the tree house, then smiled and added, "Hi, Gabriella!"

Troy and Gabriella exchanged rueful glances. They'd much rather stay in the tree house, just the two of them. But they knew that would be rude.

So, sighing, they both climbed down the tree house ladder to join the party.

CHAPTER TWO

The next morning, buses started arriving at East High School, releasing dozens of students into a new day. Other students arrived on bikes or skateboards, or had walked to school, taking advantage of the beautiful day. All of them were greeted by a new banner across the front of the building that said, CONGRATULATIONS WILDCATS BACK-TO-BACK CHAMPIONS!

The students who drove to school were angling for good spots in the parking lot. All except one. A shiny, pink convertible Mustang rode right past the student spaces and into a private spot outlined in pink right in front of the school. Sharpay Evans, Ryan's twin sister and co-president of the Drama Club, stepped out, the heels of her pink boots clattering on the pavement. But before she had taken even a few steps, two freshmen jumped forward with buckets and rags and began washing her already spotless car.

The school doors seemed to sweep open on their own as Sharpay headed inside, her long, blond hair swishing behind her. She strode down the hall without looking right or left. She didn't need to—the other students parted to make way for her, bumping into each other to get out of her path.

She breezed past a pedestal in the lobby just as Chad placed the Wildcats' new championship trophy on top of it. Troy, Zeke, and Jason grinned as the other students congratulated them.

Sharpay glanced at the group casually. "Hi,

Troy," she said. "When's the big game?"

Troy gave her a curious look. "Yesterday," he said slowly.

Sharpay looked up from checking her text messages. "Well, good luck," she replied. She continued walking down the hall.

The members of the basketball team stared after her in disbelief. How could she not know that they had played the game, that they had won, that they were champs. . . ?

But Sharpay, as usual, was totally focused on herself. She got to her locker, which was twice the size of everyone else's and painted her signature shade of pink. She glanced around to make sure no one was watching as she opened her combination lock. Suddenly she jumped, startled to find a bookish young girl with her hair pulled back, and wearing a white blouse, standing only inches away from her.

"What are *you*?" Sharpay asked. "I mean," she corrected herself, "*who* are you?"

"Good morning, Miss Evans," the girl

answered. She had a crisp British accent and a very respectful manner. "I'm Tiara Gold. I've just transferred to East High from London and noticed on the board that you were in need of a personal assistant?"

Sharpay nodded. "Well, with finals, prom, and graduation, I need someone tracking my appointments and assignments," she said grandly. "Most important, I need someone to run lines with me for the spring musical."

Sharpay then paused. Sometimes she forgot that civilians didn't know how theater people talked. She added regally, "That's a theater term for—"

"Learning your role," Tiara finished. "I understand."

She reached past Sharpay and began to re-arrange her locker, which came equipped with a pullout wardrobe rack and custom-built shelves.

"It's best to keep science and math together, since those are your first classes of the day," Tiara explained briskly.

Sharpay looked at her suspiciously and frowned. "How do you know my schedule?"

"I took the liberty of checking, simply to make certain I'd have your nonfat, no-foam soy latte ready for free period," Tiara replied. She handed Sharpay her beverage.

Sharpay's frown disappeared. "One packet of sweetener," she told Tiara.

Tiara nodded. "Organic, of course."

Sharpay raised an eyebrow. She was impressed. "I'll e-mail you my wardrobe choices each morning so that our outfits won't clash." Not that they would, Sharpay thought to herself. She doubted that Tiara had anything fabulous and pink in her closet.

She handed Tiara her book bag, relieved that she had finally found someone who clearly understood the many burdens of fame and popularity. As she walked down the hallway, it occurred to Sharpay that she should say something nice to Tiara, maybe pay her a little compliment to let her know she was appreciated.

After all, weren't the biggest stars always the nicest—*especially* when it came to the little people?

She turned her head and quickly added, "By the way, I like the accent."

Then she tossed her hair and walked away.

Troy was just about to go into homeroom. It was hard to believe, he thought, that in only a few months he would never enter Ms. Darbus's homeroom again. All of a sudden, Jimmie popped up out of nowhere. Troy jumped, surprised by the sophomore's sudden appearance, but Jimmie didn't seem to notice.

Jimmie gave Troy an excited grin. "Troy, my brother, can I have your gym locker?" he asked.

Troy's mouth dropped open. "What?" He hadn't even graduated yet, and Jimmie was already moving in on his locker?!

"Like . . . starting next week?" Jimmie suggested. "It'll help me with the guys next season if you do that."

"Why didn't I think of that?" Troy commented under his breath. Just then, the bell rang.

"Oh, man!" Jimmie cried, a panicked look on his face. "Another tardy!" He went racing down the hall.

Shaking his head, Troy went into homeroom, where the other Wildcats were already taking their seats. As Chad passed Ms. Darbus, he handed over his basketball with the resigned air of someone who has spent four years under her strict rule. She took it without a word and placed it on a special perch beside her desk, then continued distributing the printouts she was holding.

Sharpay ran into the room in a huff. When she turned to take a seat, she found Tiara right on her heels. Although she was impressed by Tiara's devotion, Sharpay realized she hadn't been quite clear about her duties. "Oh, you can go now," she said haughtily, waving a hand in dismissal.

To her surprise, Tiara didn't instantly obey

this command. "I managed to transfer into your homeroom," she explained. "Just in case I could be of service."

Sharpay gave Tiara a long, considering look. "Some people might be freaked out by you," she said. "Me . . . I like it. Take a seat."

As the students gradually took their places, still talking, Ms. Darbus called the class to order. "All right, settle down. I know we're all still excited about the Wildcats' top-to-bottom championship. . . ."

"That would be back-to-back, Miss D!" Chad called out.

Ms. Darbus sighed loudly. "In *any* case, it was a grand slam. Well done."

Troy and Chad rolled their eyes at the use of a *baseball* term to refer to their *basketball* triumph.

Ms. Darbus continued. "Now, student body president and co-editor of the yearbook, Taylor McKessie, has important announcements," she said. "Taylor?"

Immediately, Taylor stood up from her desk, grabbed a pointer, and slid a dry-erase board in front of the class. She pointed to each item written on the board in turn and said, without taking a breath, "Senior-trip subcommittee meets tomorrow and reports Thursday to prom committee, headed by Martha . . . Pick up your prom tickets from her. Graduation committee convenes Monday, following yearbook planning. Picture deadline is Thursday. Finals study groups alternate with *all* of the above. Questions?"

The class stared at her in stunned silence. Finally, Chad piped up. "What's the lunch special in the cafeteria today?" he asked jokingly.

"New York Deli," Taylor answered in a serious tone. "Anyone else?"

"Moving on," Ms. Darbus interrupted, taking the pointer away. "Sharpay Evans, four-term Drama Club co-President . . . spring musical report?" she asked.

Sharpay nodded. "With prom, finals, and

everyone being so busy, we'll select something very modest to perform. Perhaps even a one-woman show."

Ms. Darbus noticed that Kelsi Nielsen was scribbling furiously in her notebook. "A little light on the sign-ups, Kelsi?" she inquired.

Kelsi barely looked up and continued writing in her notebook. "Oh, no, actually we're doing pretty well . . ."

Ms. Darbus walked over to Kelsi and grabbed her clipboard. "Well, well, well . . . almost the entire homeroom. How inspiring!" she exclaimed.

Everyone in the class turned to look at each other, puzzled. They didn't *remember* signing up for the spring musical auditions.

Sharpay's mouth dropped open in disbelief. She thought she'd made it clear last year that no one should ever again consider encroaching on her territory, which was the theater and everything that took place in it.

Every eye turned toward Kelsi, who lowered

the brim of her hat and slid down in her seat.

"So, I'll be seeing all of you during free period to discuss the show," Ms. Darbus went on, unaware of the tension in the room. "*And* for a *very* special announcement—"

As usual, Ms. Darbus's timing was perfect. The bell rang before anyone could respond. Everybody began gathering their notebooks to head for their next class. As Chad passed Ms. Darbus, she handed him back his basketball.

Troy sighed. "Leave it to Darbus to make free period mandatory."

When the bell rang announcing free period, Sharpay was the first person at the theater and onstage. She was pacing back and forth. A protesting crowd of Wildcats surrounded Kelsi, who was sitting at the piano.

"I'll be retaking my finals two or three times. I'm moving into the library," Jason told her.

"Kels, I was going to be using free period to work on my truck," Troy said.

"I've got five new recipes to nail for my Family Science final," Zeke added.

Taylor looked over at Gabriella. "We've got a yearbook to edit. So no can do."

Kelsi looked crestfallen. "Sorry," she said quietly. "I just thought since it was the last show, everyone would want to do it."

Gabriella hadn't yet said anything. She chose this moment to step forward. "Hey, listen up. Kelsi's right. We should do this." She looked around at her friends. "Jason—Taylor, Martha, and I can help you study. Zeke—we're your official tasters. This is our last chance to do something together, all of us. Something really fun."

From her spot at center stage, Sharpay had been following the debate with interest and delight. So no one wants to be in the musical, she thought, smiling to herself. But now, she could tell that Gabriella's emotional appeal was working. She frowned.

"Oh, yippie," she muttered under her breath.

She could just imagine it: friendship and fun and high spirits . . . in *her* theater! Where there was supposed to be drama and discipline and one—count her, *one*—diva!

Still, there was a chance that Gabriella's argument might fail. Taylor, for example, seemed skeptical.

"But how much time will it take?" Taylor asked.

"And what is the show about?" Chad questioned.

A voice from somewhere behind them said, "You, Mr. Danforth."

They turned to see Ms. Darbus, holding her clipboard, striding down the aisle toward them. "The spring musical," she said grandly, "is all about . . . *you*."

"*Me?*" Chad sounded surprised—and alarmed.

He wasn't the only one.

Up on the stage, Sharpay fainted.

When Sharpay came to a few moments later, she

found that Tiara was gently spritzing her face with a spray bottle filled with mineral water to revive her. She sat up groggily.

Ms. Darbus, who knew a hysterical faint when she saw one, continued without missing a beat. "It's about *all* of you. And all of you will create it . . . a show about your last days at East High. We'll call it"—she paused dramatically, as if trying to find the perfect name—"*Senior Year.*"

The Wildcats looked at each other. *Senior Year*? *That* was the name of their musical?

Chad shrugged and kept spinning his basketball. He didn't care *what* the musical was called. All he cared about was not getting onstage and singing. *Ever.*

"Kelsi will compose, Ryan choreograph . . . and I'll do my best to guide you," Ms. Darbus announced, trying to sound modest.

She then looked at the group intently. "Now, important news from The Juilliard School in New York City, America's preeminent college for the performing arts. Yes, for the first time in East

High history, four of you are being considered for one available theater arts scholarship." She looked at the seniors proudly.

She held up a letter. "Yes, Juilliard is considering Miss Sharpay Evans . . ."

Sharpay beamed. "I'm already packed."

Ms. Darbus continued, "Mr. Ryan Evans . . ."

Ryan did a blazing five-second tap dance out of sheer joy.

"Miss Kelsi Nielsen . . ."

Kelsi's eyes opened wide with shock. "Whoa," she said softly. "They got my letter."

"Indeed they did," Ms. Darbus said, smiling. "And finally . . . Mr. Troy Bolton."

Every head swiveled to stare at Troy. He grinned back. After all, this was all a big joke . . . wasn't it?

"Juilliard will send representatives to observe our spring show. So . . . good luck to our four applicants," Ms. Darbus said.

The Drama Club teacher didn't sound like she was joking, but Troy was laughing as he asked his friends, "All right . . . who's the big comedian?" He pointed to Gabriella. "Ha, ha, ha."

Gabriella shrugged. She was as surprised as he was.

Troy turned to Chad. "Pretty good, dude."

But Chad just shook his head. He loved jokes, and this was a good one. He would have been proud to call it his own, except for one thing—he had nothing to do with it.

"Is there something wrong?" Ms. Darbus was a little disappointed at Troy's reaction.

"I didn't apply," he explained. "I've never heard of . . . Juilliard."

"Well, that may be, Mr. Bolton," she said crisply. "But, evidently, Juilliard has heard of *you*."

She focused her attention back to the spring musical. Her gaze swept the group standing in front of her. "And as you create this show, then you must dig down and think about your aspirations, your dreams for the future.

Line up, please. Let's begin with Mr. Danforth."

Chad looked at Ms. Darbus blankly. Was she seriously asking Chad what his dreams were? He had only had the same dream since he was ten years old, and everyone knew what it was. Chad spun his basketball to give Ms. Darbus a clue. "My dreams? U of A. Hoops all the way."

Ms. Darbus smiled. "Miss McKessie?"

"*My* future?" Taylor asked. "I'd like to be president of the United States." She paused, smiling happily at the daydream that constantly ran through her mind—whenever she wasn't studying, of course.

"Do we get extra credit for just . . . like . . . showing up?" Jason wanted to know.

Ms. Darbus quietly groaned and turned to Kelsi, waiting for her response to the question.

"To write some songs we'll remember . . ." she replied wistfully.

Just then, Martha came hurrying into the theater.

"Martha Cox, you're late!" Ms Darbus shouted.

Martha tried to catch her breath. "I had my American Folk Dance class . . . and thought maybe we could use a few more dancers . . ."

"I'm feeling a show already!" Ms. Darbus exclaimed, her eyes sparkling with excitement. "Troy Bolton?"

But Troy wasn't in a theatrical mood. "To bust whoever signed me up for this!" he said loudly.

Ms. Darbus sighed. "And Miss Montez?" she asked.

"I think we should stage the perfect prom," Gabriella replied.

Sharpay rolled her eyes. "That's *adorable*," she commented. "What do *I* want? Gosh, I wouldn't know where to begin . . . but I know where it ends." She imagined herself stepping into a spotlight. "Center stage, a single spotlight . . . a huge marquee that reads—"

She swept her hand through the air. No one had any doubts about what she was seeing.

Her name. In lights.

But by lunchtime, the only marquee was the one in the cafeteria. And the only words on it were NEW YORK DELI PLATTER, which meant corned beef on rye, Swiss cheese, potato salad, pickles, and a "Big Apple" parfait, the dessert of the day. In addition to the lunch menu, the sign said, PICK UP YOUR PROM TICKETS TODAY!

Sharpay and Ryan stood in line with their lunch trays. When it was Ryan's turn to order, he said, "I'll have the New York Deli Platter, please, double cheese. And throw in that "Big Apple" parfait . . . if they make it there, I'll eat it any-where."

Sharpay gave her brother a disapproving look. "How can you think about food at a time like *this*?" she demanded.

"Maybe because it's lunchtime," Ryan sug-gested.

"I'm talking about the show, Ryan!" Sharpay barked.

Sharpay led the way to the second level of

the cafeteria, with Tiara behind them, carrying Sharpay's lunch tray. As they walked, Sharpay continued talking. "That puppy dog Troy Bolton *pretended* to know nothing about Juilliard." She gave a small snort.

Sharpay and Ryan sat in their usual spot, which was empty and waiting for them thanks to the pink RESERVED sign displayed on the table. Tiara began setting Sharpay's place as Ryan said, "Troy looked genuinely surprised."

"Oh, so the theater fairy *magically* sent in Troy's application?" Sharpay scoffed. "Performers can't fool me, Ryan. They're deceitful, ambitious, and ruthless."

Ryan took a bite of his sandwich and chewed thoughtfully. Then he asked, "Aren't *we* . . . performers?"

Sharpay nodded, glad that Ryan had grasped her point. "Exactly!" she exclaimed.

She said it with such conviction, such absolute, unshakeable faith in their destiny, that Ryan couldn't help but be swayed. Sharpay was right! he thought. They *both* belonged at Juilliard—no matter what it took to get there.

He suddenly frowned as he remembered one important minor detail.

"Wait a minute . . . Ms. D. said there's only one scholarship available," Ryan pointed out.

Sharpay waved one hand dismissively. "We're twins," she said. "They'll have to take us both."

Ryan tried to understand this logic, but Sharpay was already moving on to the first step in her scheme. "Kelsi always writes her best songs for Troy and Gabriella," she said. "So you make certain *we* get those songs."

"How?" he asked.

"Polish her glasses. Buy her some ruby slippers," Sharpay snapped impatiently. "I don't know. Just do it!"

CHAPTER THREE

"Coming to rehearsal today?" Gabriella asked Taylor the next morning as they got off the bus in front of school.

Taylor rolled her eyes. "Do I have a choice? You got us into this." She gave Gabriella a puzzled look. "Which I don't understand. Have you even told *anyone* you're up for Stanford's freshman honors program?"

Gabriella shook her head. Only her mother and Taylor knew that she might be able to start college early—even before she graduated from high school. Not only had she not told anyone else, but she was trying to forget all about the possibility herself.

"You're going to be hearing from them any day," Taylor told her.

Gabriella looked down. "I already heard from them," she admitted.

Just then, Gabriella's cell phone rang, and Troy's face appeared on the screen. She answered the call. "Look up," he said.

"Huh?" Gabriella tilted her head back and blinked in astonishment. Troy was waving from the rooftop of the school!

"Gotta go!" Gabriella told Taylor, hurrying away.

Taylor gave Gabriella a look that said their conversation was far from over.

Gabriella rushed inside East High and began climbing the stairs that led to Troy's secret hideaway: a rooftop oasis of flowers and vegetables maintained by the Garden Club.

When Gabriella reached the top, she opened the door to the roof and found Troy standing near a trellis, which had three tuxedos hanging from it.

"You've got to help me with this," he said, grinning. "Which one should I wear?" he asked.

She smiled. "Because . . . ?" she asked.

"You're going to have a beautiful dress, and I want to look right," he explained.

Gabriella's face glowed. "I've never been asked to a prom, but this almost sounds like an invitation."

Troy reached into one of the tuxedo jackets and pulled out two tickets with the words EAST HIGH SENIOR PROM—LAST WALTZ printed on them.

Gabriella looked over at the tickets and smiled. She took a tuxedo jacket from the rack and helped him put it on over his T-shirt.

"Will we have to waltz?" Troy asked lightly, trying to cover up how nervous he felt. "I really don't know how to do that."

"All I know is what my dad showed me when I

was a little girl," Gabriella said wistfully. "I'd stand on his toes, and he'd waltz me around the living room."

She looked over at Troy and gave him a shy glance. "Come here," she said.

They began dancing, awkwardly at first, as they tried to teach each other the steps. Soon, however, they were moving gracefully around the roof, smiling and gazing into each other's eyes. A light rain began to fall, but that didn't stop them. Waltzing, as it turned out, was too much fun.

Finally, they took a break.

"Is that a yes?" Troy asked.

"Yes," Gabriella replied.

As they happily looked at each other, the bell suddenly rang, forcing them to dash for the stairwell. Talking about the prom would have to wait until later.

Troy was still in a good mood later that afternoon when he headed for the gym. He spotted

Jimmie and Donny stepping out of the shower area, wrapped in towels but still dripping wet. He grinned as he watched them reach their lockers and suddenly realize they were mysteriously open. *And* empty.

Troy paused for a few seconds to enjoy their confused expressions, then called out, "Yo, Rocketman . . ."

The two sophomores whirled around to see Troy and Chad leaning against a locker partition, holding Jimmie's and Donny's clothes.

"You guys wanted our lockers?" Troy asked.

"Well, it's moving day!" Chad announced.

Jimmie brightened immediately. "Sweet!"

Troy and Chad began walking toward the area where the varsity team's lockers were, closely followed by Jimmie and Donny. Troy counted the steps in his head—five, six, seven—then glanced over at Chad.

Suddenly, they both took off running, still carrying Jimmie's and Donny's things!

The two sophomores clutched their towels

more tightly and gave chase through the Hall of Champions. When Donny saw that they were headed for the main hall, he yelled, "Hey, joke's over, guys!"

But Troy and Chad didn't stop. As students hooted and cheered, they raced through the hall, still pursued by Jimmie and Donny. The two boys were so intent on catching Troy and Chad they didn't even notice that they were being led toward the theater. Troy and Chad burst through a door, and Jimmie and Donny went flying right in after them—and suddenly found themselves onstage!

Center stage, in fact.

Holding their towels and still dripping wet.

The auditorium went silent as the students who were painting sets and studying scripts stopped what they were doing to gape at the scene. Kelsi even stopped playing the piano.

"Yearbook opportunity," Gabriella murmured to Taylor.

Taylor had already had the same thought. She

nodded to the yearbook photographer who snapped a quick photo. "Got it!"

Ms. Darbus, who was used to improvisation and theatrical mishaps, took the situation in stride. "Bold choice, gentlemen, bold choice," she commented. "We must *all* have the courage to discover ourselves. However, at East High, we'll discover ourselves while clothed. But welcome to our spring musical," she said dryly. "And on with the show," she added.

Later that afternoon, Troy and Gabriella pulled up in front of Gabriella's house in his truck. It came to a lurching stop.

"If my truck falls apart because I'm spending my free time onstage, it's all on you," Troy said, pretending to complain.

"*Me*?" Gabriella protested playfully.

"You think I'd be up there if it wasn't for you?" he joked.

She smiled at him for a moment before she answered, "Yeah, I do."

They hopped out of the truck and entered Gabriella's backyard. She turned and gave Troy a serious look.

"Troy, I watch you in rehearsal," she said. "You love it. Why is that so hard for you to admit?"

Troy looked sheepish. It was still difficult for him to believe how much he had changed since he had met Gabriella. A year ago, he didn't even know where the theater *was*, and he had never hung out with kids from the Drama Club—let alone tried out for a musical. But now . . . she was right. He did love it. Was it hard to admit that? Well . . .

"It isn't to you," he said. "But to my dad? To Chad? Yeah, that's a little hard."

"It shouldn't be," Gabriella told him.

Troy took a deep breath. It felt great being able to talk about everything he'd been feeling lately . . . especially with Gabriella. "They're happy as long as we're all talking about U of A. *You* chose Stanford . . . U of A was sort of chosen *for* me," he revealed. "I haven't been talking about this with anyone . . . but I've had offers from other colleges. And I'm really listening."

Gabriella looked at Troy sympathetically. "I get it, Troy. I've still got decisions to make, too."

"Like what?" Troy asked, surprised.

She opened her mouth to speak, but her mother chose that very moment to walk out onto Gabriella's balcony.

"I've got snacks for you inside . . ." she began. Mrs. Montez looked down at her daughter and Troy and noticed their serious expressions. "I think I interrupted something," she said slowly.

"Just talking, Mom," Gabriella replied quietly.

After all, there would be plenty of time to talk to Troy about everything later, she thought.

CHAPTER FOUR

The next morning, Gabriella and Taylor met to work on the East High yearbook. On the computer, they clicked through action shots from the Wildcats' championship game and laid out pages as other yearbook staffers worked at their own desks.

A little while later, they were interrupted by Troy and Chad, who arrived with brownies. Gabriella reached out to grab one and said teasingly, "Kissing up to the yearbook editors. *Very* smart move."

"Chad's hoping for two pages for himself," Troy joked. "Maybe even a third page, just for his hair."

"Hey, what's right is right," Chad said, grinning. He looked at Troy as if suddenly struck by a thought. "Hoops, by the way, you've got to take me after school to check out the whole tuxedo thing."

Troy and Gabriella exchanged glances. "I'm definitely an expert," he said, smiling.

"Tuxedo?" Taylor asked. "What for?"

"Um . . . prom?" Chad answered.

Every other girl in the room turned to look at Chad with hopeful looks in their eyes.

Taylor, however, just lifted one mocking eyebrow and met Chad's gaze with a direct one of her own. "Honey, if that's what you call a formal invitation, you'll be dancing with yourself," she said haughtily.

She poked the basketball he was carrying

under his arm, and it went rolling out into the hallway.

Meanwhile, Zeke and Jason were walking toward Sharpay's backstage dressing room. Zeke was a bundle of nerves, but Jason prodded him along and nudged him up the stairs.

Inside Sharpay's dressing room, Tiara was going through a box of photos. Tiara held up one picture at a time for Sharpay's approval, dropping the "yes's" into a box for the yearbook staff and the "no's" into a box labeled EAST HIGH ARCHIVES.

"Yes," Sharpay said in response to a photo. "No . . . No . . . Yes . . . No . . ." She paused, then asked, "How many have I approved?"

Tiara knew the number without even checking. "Sixty-seven," she said confidently.

"That'll do," Sharpay said crisply. "Deliver those to the yearbook room."

Suddenly, a very nervous Zeke appeared in the doorway.

"Um . . . Sharpay . . . there's something I've been wanting to ask you for about a year . . ." he began haltingly. Even to his own ears, he sounded totally nervous. Fortunately, that didn't matter—because Sharpay wasn't even listening.

"Oh, Zeke, glad you stopped by," she said breezily. "You're taking me to prom. Don't buy a corsage, it's being flown in from Hawaii."

"I've sent the florist a fabric swatch," Tiara told Sharpay, her voice brisk and efficient.

Sharpay nodded, pleased, and went on, "Daddy will arrange limousine and restaurant."

Tiara stepped forward and began measuring Zeke's shoulders and arms.

"Your tuxedo will be delivered, but don't wear it to your ballroom-dance lessons," Sharpay added.

"Dance lessons?" Zeke asked. He looked dazed.

"Beginning Monday," Sharpay said. "Questions? No? Good. Toodles!"

Before he knew it, Zeke was headed back

down the stairs, still shocked by his encounter with Sharpay. Jason was waiting for him at the foot of the stairs, wearing a T-shirt with the words JASON + MARTHA = PROM printed on the front.

Jason eyed Zeke closely. He really hoped that Zeke's mission to ask Sharpay had succeeded. Maybe, he thought, it will be a good omen for when I approach Martha . . .

"Well?" Jason asked eagerly.

Zeke gave him a weak smile. "I didn't even give her a chance to say no."

Troy saw Chad enter the cafeteria, a preoccupied look on his face. Before approaching him, Troy glanced around the room. At every table, clusters of students caught his eye and then quickly looked away.

Troy grinned. Perfect! Everything had been set up; now he just needed to put the plan into action.

He caught up with Chad and nudged him with

his elbow, then pointed at the table where Taylor was sitting with Gabriella, Kelsi, and Martha.

"Now or never, dude," Troy said.

Chad looked nervous, but determined. "Okay, okay," he said. "I'm going in."

Troy reached into his backpack and pulled out a bunch of flowers cut from the rooftop garden. In one smooth motion, he took the basketball out of Chad's hand and replaced it with the bouquet. "The Garden Club is rooting for you," he told Chad.

Chad did not seem very reassured by the news, but he nodded and walked toward Taylor's table.

Without even saying hello, he blurted out, "So, anyway, I was really hoping you'd kind of go to the prom with me."

Troy bit his lip to keep from laughing. Smooth, Chad, he thought. *Real* smooth.

However, it seemed that Taylor hadn't even heard his clumsy attempt at an invitation. Or else she was pretending that she didn't hear. She glanced up at Chad and said, "Oh, hi, Chad. Hey, they've got Tuna Surprise on the menu. Your favorite."

"The prom," Chad said a little more louder. "I'm asking you."

Taylor shook her head, frowning slightly. "It's so loud in here," she said. "You'll have to speak up."

This was it! Troy raised his arm and the entire cafeteria fell silent just as Chad dropped to one knee and shouted, "Taylor McKessie, will you *please* be my date to the senior prom?"

For a long moment, Taylor just looked at him. Then she looked at her friends. Then she looked back at Chad.

"I'd be honored," she announced.

At that moment, the cafeteria burst into applause and cheers.

Troy patted Chad on the back and handed him his basketball.

"Dude, I need to go shoot some hoops," Chad said, who was very relieved his ordeal was over. "Right away," he added.

Fifteen minutes later, they were still dressed

in their street clothes finishing a game of H-O-R-S-E in the gym. Troy took his turn and made a basket with ease. "Horse!" he called out.

"Go again?" Chad asked.

Troy shook his head. He knew what Chad was avoiding. As his best friend, Troy couldn't let him do it. "Dude, we can shoot hoops all day, but we still got to get you into a tuxedo," he said. "No way out, man."

A little while later, back in the theater, Ms. Darbus was commenting on the Wildcats' rehearsal. "Kelsi, the music is splendid, Ryan, your choreography is most inventive," Ms. Darbus began. She looked over at Jason and scowled. "Jason, we don't chew gum in the theater. . . ."

Chastened, Jason took the gum out of his mouth and put it in his shirt pocket.

Sharpay grabbed Ryan's arm and nodded toward Kelsi. "I heard she's writing something amazing for Troy and Gabriella."

"A song, most likely," Ryan said mildly.

Sharpay's grip tightened. "Find out what it is!" she hissed.

She nudged Ryan toward the piano. He stumbled right in front of Kelsi, who was gathering her sheet music.

"So, hey, how can we make this whole show better?" he asked, fumbling for words as Sharpay glared at him. "Maybe we could get together?"

"I'm in the music room every morning as soon as they unlock the school," Kelsi said. "Actually, I have my own key, but don't tell anyone," she said shyly. "It's really early but . . . I do have a teapot. Come on by!"

Ryan smiled. That was pretty easy, he thought. Even if Sharpay *had*—literally—pushed him into it.

On the other side of the stage, Jimmie suddenly popped up in front of Troy. Troy jumped in surprise. Jimmie always seemed to startle him.

"Hey, good job, Troy!" Jimmie exclaimed.

"Stop *doing* that!" Troy told him, a little annoyed that Jimmie had caught him off guard. *Again.* He glanced around the theater, wondering if there was some way he could slip away. Once Jimmie started talking, he never seemed to want to stop.

"Look, there's Sharpay!" Troy exclaimed. "You didn't hear this from me, but she has a secret crush on you," he then whispered to Jimmie.

Jimmie's face lit up. He swiveled around to look at Sharpay. Troy saw his chance to escape, and he took it.

As Jimmie headed in Sharpay's direction, Ms. Darbus grabbed him. "Mr. Zara?" she asked.

"Call me Rocketman if you want to," Jimmie answered.

"How generous," Ms. Darbus replied sarcastically. "And since you've been such a . . . dedicated presence here, I'm making you an understudy." She nodded toward Tiara, who had been hanging out at rehearsal every day, too. She had been running errands for

Sharpay, bringing her cups of tea, and acting like the most efficient personal assistant in the world. Perhaps it was time, Ms. Darbus thought, to redirect that energy a bit. Say, toward the last production of the season. "Tiara, you as well."

"I'm in!" Jimmie pumped his fist in triumph and called out to his friend Donny, who was standing nearby. "Hey, Donny, I'm IN!!! I'm playing understudy."

Donny looked impressed. "Way cool. You rock, Jimmie Z!"

Tiara rolled her eyes. "Understudy isn't a role, you morons," she whispered. "It means you go on if one of the leads can't make it for the performance."

"Oh." Jimmie's face fell. "Well, you're one, too."

Tiara tossed her head. "The difference being, *I* can actually carry a tune."

"Hey, I wouldn't sing with you if my hair was on fire and you were the last bucket of water on Earth," Jimmie replied.

"And I wouldn't sing with you if I were starving and you were the last pickle at the picnic," Tiara said huffily.

They eyed each other for a long, interested moment.

"Want to have lunch sometime?" Jimmie asked.

Tiara smiled briefly and then walked away. She had already learned from Sharpay that it's always best to make a dramatic exit.

Later that day, Gabriella and Taylor were back in the yearbook room, working on their layouts. Gabriella seemed uncharacteristically subdued. Finally, she reached into her backpack and handed a letter to Taylor.

Taylor began to read the letter aloud. "Stanford University's freshman honors program cordially . . ." She stopped reading and reached out to give Gabriella a hug.

"Just tell me you've already said yes . . . right?" Taylor asked.

Gabriella shook her head. "I haven't even told my mom I got the letter."

Taylor gave Gabriella her patented "Taylor look." The one that meant, "I can't *believe* you just said that!"

Gabriella was about to respond, but instinct made her glance at the door instead. She saw Tiara standing there, holding the box of Sharpay's "approved" photos and smiling innocently.

Gabriella bit her lip. Tiara had obviously been standing there for a while. How much had she overheard?

Tiara stared intently at the monitor at one of the library's computer workstations. As she surfed the Internet, Sharpay leaned over her shoulder and peered closely at the screen.

At first, there were images of Stanford University. A few clicks later, and a photo of Gabriella, along with several other students, appeared. The headline on the page announced:

The seniors are graduating from East High and can't wait for the spring musical, prom, and graduation!

It's the championship game against West High and the Wildcats are losing. Troy and Chad get ready to psych the team up.

The pressure is on.

The Wildcats make a spectacular comeback
and win the game!

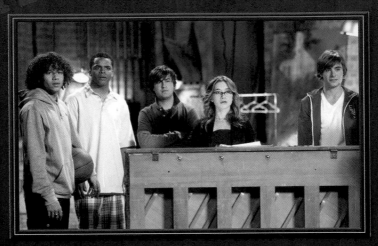

When Ms. Darbus announces that this year's musical will be all about the graduating seniors, the Wildcats are shocked.

Sharpay faints when she finds out the theme of the spring musical. Luckily, her personal assistant, Tiara Gold, is there to catch her!

As graduation nears, Troy and Gabriella reflect on the wonderful times they've had together at East High.

Troy debates whether he should tell his dad that he may not want to attend the University of Albuquerque.

Gabriella wonders whether she should attend the freshman honors program at Stanford University.

Troy surprises Gabriella the night of the East High prom, and they waltz around the quad at Stanford. It's a night to remember!

The rest of the Wildcats dance the night away at their prom at East High.

Wildcats forever!

STANFORD UNIVERSITY FRESHMAN HONOREES.

Tiara looked impressed. "They select only thirty freshmen from the entire incoming class," she explained to Sharpay. "It's a special three-week honors program."

"How prestigious," Sharpay quipped sarcastically.

Tiara scrolled down to read more. "But the program starts in two weeks!" she exclaimed. "She'd miss our"—she caught herself—"*your* show."

"Oh, my goodness!" Sharpay said in mock despair. "What to do?"

Sharpay smiled smugly as the beginning of a scheme began to form in her mind. "Well, the show must go on . . . mustn't it?"

CHAPTER FIVE

Ryan arrived at East High very early the next morning. He looked around the courtyard. It was eerily empty at this hour, with no crowds of students, no laughing, no jostling, no yelling . . .

In fact, he thought, it was a rather nice change.

He went inside and made his way to the music room. As he slipped inside, he noticed the morning light streaming through the windows, casting a glow around the grand piano, kettle drums, music stands . . . and Kelsi, who was perched on top of a piano and looking out the window, lost in thought.

He sat down quietly at the grand piano. The music sheet in front of him read, "Just Want to Be with You," Kelsi Nielsen . . . duet Troy/Gabriella." He began picking out part of the melody on the piano. Kelsi turned around, and he smiled at her.

"Kind of beautiful," he said, giving her a shy smile.

She shrugged, but she looked pleased. "Stuck on the bridge," she admitted. "Worried about the show . . ."

"Shouldn't be," he said. "It's sounding good. The prom number was great. So is this one."

He continued playing for a moment. Then he looked at her and asked, "So . . . what are you doing prom night?"

"It's two days before the show," she replied. "I'll be working on charts and fixing orchestrations and probably changing song lyrics right up until—"

"Good," Ryan interrupted. "Pick you up at eight."

It took Kelsi a moment to understand what Ryan had just said—but when she did, she gave him a big smile. Then she sat on the piano bench beside him, and they finished playing the song as a duet.

A few hours later, Kelsi was still playing the same song, but now she was in the theater's orchestra pit with the rhythm section. Other students were also there rehearsing. The set was a house with a balcony—one that looked remarkably like the balcony at Gabriella's house—and a large tree that "grew" right out of the orchestra pit. Gabriella was sitting on the balcony, and Troy was climbing the tree to reach her as Ryan, Sharpay, and Ms. Darbus watched.

Troy and Gabriella sang the song Kelsi

wrote for them with great emotion. As the last notes of "Just Want to Be with You" drifted away, Ryan told them, "Pity the actor who has to follow that in the show." He stopped, struck by a dismaying thought. "Wait. It might be me."

Gabriella smiled warmly at him. "The way you dance, you've got no worries."

"Yeah, we're all trying to catch up with you," Troy added.

Ryan felt a glow of happiness—not just because of the compliments, but because he really loved being around his friends. Last year, he would never have imagined in his wildest dreams that a brainiac like Gabriella or a jock like Troy would be his friends. But now . . .

"Ryan?" Sharpay's voice sliced through his thoughts.

Sighing, he walked over to where his sister was standing in the wings.

"Did you get a copy of that song from Kelsi?" she asked.

"No, but I'm taking her to the prom!" Ryan exclaimed.

"Brilliant!" Sharpay looked more pleased with this news than he would have expected. He understood why when she added, "Keep your friends close and your enemies closer. Now, get me that duet."

"Um . . ." Ryan hesitated, a little scared to say what he was thinking. Then he took a deep breath and said bravely, "Last time I checked, you're not Gabriella."

To his surprise, Sharpay didn't yell at him for this tiny insubordination. She didn't scream. She didn't even frown. Instead, she looked smug.

"Don't be so sure," she told Ryan, as she turned to walk backstage.

Later that afternoon, Taylor was at Gabriella's house. They had yearbook materials spread out all over Gabriella's bedroom, and Gabriella was doing her best to concentrate on the work they had to do. But Taylor couldn't focus. They had something they needed to talk about, and she wasn't going to let the yearbook get in the way.

"You should be throwing a party, not keeping a secret," Taylor told her firmly.

"But it starts at Stanford next week!" Gabriella cried. They had gone over this a hundred times. Why couldn't Taylor understand? She tried one more time to make her position clear. "I'll miss everything!"

"You'll come back for prom and graduation," Taylor countered. "You had enough credits to graduate from East High last December. Sister, your future is calling, loud and clear."

Gabriella sighed with frustration. "Stop being my mom for a second and just be my friend!" she protested. "Maybe I like it here. Maybe I want to stay in Albuquerque as long as possible."

She paused and then decided to finally open up and say the thing she had barely let herself think about, the thing that she knew would shock Taylor more than anything else. "Maybe I'll just stay *here* next year."

Sure enough, Taylor's eyes opened wide. "WHAT?!!!"

While Gabriella and Taylor were having a heart-to-heart, Troy and Chad were bouncing down a back road in Troy's beat-up truck. They finally came to a halt at a junkyard filled with rusted old cars and trucks in various stages of disrepair. A basketball hoop was nailed up on the fence, and the rough markings of a basketball court were outlined in the dirt.

Mr. Riley, the junkyard's owner, sauntered over to the truck.

"My fuel pump is deceased, Mr. Riley," Troy said ruefully.

Mr. Riley grinned. "Dig around, you'll find one here. Can't wait to see you guys play for U of A next year. Already bought my season tickets." He tossed Chad the keys to the gate. "Lock up when you leave."

Troy and Chad opened the gate and walked over to a giant pile of spare parts. They began searching for a fuel pump.

"Hear that?" Chad asked. "Season tickets. Time to start practicing, dude."

"Take a breather, LeBron," Troy said as he dug through the pile. "Man, don't you ever feel like your entire life is already being laid out for you?"

Chad gave him a puzzled look. "What's your point?"

"I just want my future to be . . . *my* future," Troy said.

"See what happens when you do a show?" Chad asked jokingly. "You're like . . . five people."

Troy bristled a bit, even though he knew Chad was just teasing. "What's so bad about that?" he asked. "When we used to come here as kids, we'd be ten people! Spies, superheroes, rock stars . . . we were whatever we wanted to be, whenever we wanted to be it. It was us, man!"

"We were eight years old," Chad pointed out. Then he grinned. "And for the record, I was a *much* better superhero than you."

He snatched up a piece of metal and brandished it like a sword. Troy laughed and grabbed a piece of his own. Suddenly, they were both acting like kids, jumping from car to car, sword fighting among the piles of rusty parts. They were laughing so hard they were doubled over. It was almost as if they were replaying every moment from their years of friendship. And they were having a blast doing it.

Finally, they stopped and tried to catch their breath. They stood next to each other in the approaching dusk, still panting.

Gradually, boyhood slipped away once more, and the future loomed on the horizon again, both tantalizing and terrifying.

"What are you going to do if Juilliard says yes?" Chad asked.

"I don't know," Troy admitted.

Chad's high spirits fell a bit. "That's not what

I wanted to hear," he said. "I'm getting you back in the gym tomorrow."

He shoved Troy playfully, and they piled into the truck, ready to go home.

Back at Gabriella's house, Taylor was shocked at what Gabriella had just told her.

"Stay in Albuquerque?" Taylor gasped. "That makes no sense."

She was sitting on the bed in Gabriella's room, trying to recover from what her friend had just said.

"And why do I always have to make sense?" Gabriella argued. "I'll still go to Stanford. But maybe in a year. I can take classes at U of A. I don't know."

"U of A?" Taylor couldn't believe what she was hearing. "You're not thinking clearly, because you're thinking about Troy. He's your first crush. But there'll be more boys, more Troys."

Gabriella turned around and spotted her mother standing in the doorway. Great! First she had Taylor on her case. Now she was going to have to explain herself to her mother.

Gabriella couldn't deal with that right then. She ran out onto the balcony to be by herself.

Mrs. Montez and Taylor exchanged identical, and worried, glances.

They both wanted what was best for Gabriella—but would she be able to see that?

Later that evening, the Bolton and Danforth families were having a celebration dinner at Troy's house. Chad was proudly wearing his new U of A jersey. Troy was trying to put up a good front, but he really wasn't feeling that festive.

"First U of A game is at home against Trinity," Troy's dad said. "But the next game is away . . . against Tulane."

"That's New Orleans, right?" Mrs. Bolton asked.

"Road trip!" Mr. Danforth exclaimed. He gave Troy's dad a high five.

Troy smiled weakly. He wished he could be as

excited as everyone else was. But he was just so confused. He knew he had to make a decision about college. And soon.

Gabriella was still on her balcony, looking up at the starry night sky, when her mother opened the door and stepped out.

Her mother looked at Gabriella with concern. "High school feels like the most important thing in the world. When you're in it. But that changes," she said gently.

"Not everything has to change, Mom," Gabriella said. "I don't believe that."

Mrs. Montez knew what Gabriella was feeling. She also knew enough to stop talking. She just gave her daughter a quick hug and went back inside.

Dinner was finished at the Bolton house. The Danforths had gone home, and Troy's parents were clearing the kitchen. Troy was out in the backyard, shooting hoops. He stopped for a moment to watch his parents through the window. It was a familiar scene. His mom and dad smiled and talked softly to each other as they put the dishes away, the same way they had for as long as he could remember.

He looked away from them. That was becoming a part of his past now. Pretty soon, he wouldn't be living here, wouldn't be having dinner at home almost every night, and wouldn't be watching his parents do the same things that he had long ago started taking for granted.

He put his basketball on the ground and headed toward his treehouse. He climbed up the stairs and then stared up at the sky. The stars looked even more distant and unreachable than usual—as distant and unreachable as his own future. Without quite realizing it, he began to sing a few bars of "Right Here, Right Now," another song that Kelsi wrote for the musical, the tempo slow and meditative. . . .

A few miles away, Gabriella was by herself on

her balcony, singing the same song. Despite all the confusion she was feeling, singing made her feel calm—almost as if Troy were sitting beside her and singing, too.

Together, Troy and Gabriella sang a duet without even knowing it.

Or, maybe, in some way, they did.

CHAPTER SIX

The next morning, Gabriella was standing at her locker, organizing her books for the day, when Troy slid around the corner. He pulled out his cell phone and began scrolling through photos of flowers.

"Okay, prom corsages," he said, holding out the phone so Gabriella could see a picture of each flower as it came up on the screen. "Take your pick, because if you leave it up to me . . . well . . ."

"If you pick it out, I'm going to like it,"

78

Gabriella said. She took another look at the corsages and added with a laugh, "Unless it's that one."

Suddenly, the bell rang. They smiled at each other and headed off to their separate classes.

Later that day, Troy was at his locker gathering his books. He closed the locker door and was startled to see Sharpay standing there.

"Hi, Troy!" Sharpay said brightly. "I realized I haven't offered my congratulations."

"Thanks, but to tell you the truth, I'm glad the season's over," Troy replied politely.

"I didn't mean basketball, silly," she said with a mischievous grin. "I meant Gabriella."

"Huh?" Troy asked.

Sharpay gave Troy a serious look. "Her missing the show is a little disappointing. But being selected for Stanford's freshman honors program . . . well, that's amazing for her."

Troy looked at her in confusion. "I don't know what you're talking about," he said.

"Everyone else does," Sharpay said matter-of-factly. "The whole school is buzzing. The honorees get to spend time with Stanford's top professors in special classes. Starting next week."

"Next week?" Troy asked in surprise.

Sharpay looked at him pitifully. "You *really* didn't know?" she asked. "Okay, this is a little awkward. I guess her not telling you means she's on the fence about it. But who better than Troy Bolton to encourage her to accept that honor, since the only thing possibly holding her back is . . . you."

With that, Sharpay walked off, leaving a dumbfounded Troy standing at his locker.

That night, Gabriella was doing homework in her room when her cell phone rang. She answered distractedly and heard a strange voice say, "Pizza's here."

She frowned. "I didn't order pizza," she told the caller.

Then she heard Troy, using his regular voice, say, "You didn't have to."

Smiling, she stepped out onto the balcony and into the warm night air. She turned to see him standing in the backyard, holding a pizza box.

He looked at Gabriella and grinned. "Half vegetarian, half everything else. Oh, and let's not forget—"

He put the box down and grabbed the rope that was hanging over the balcony. He pulled up a box that was rigged to the rope and added, "What's a picnic without chocolate-covered strawberries?"

Gabriella shook her head, giggling. "You are one crazy Wildcat."

Troy climbed up the tree near Gabriella's balcony, while Gabriella hoisted up the basket from the ground and then began laying out their food. Fifteen minutes later, they had worked their way through half the pizza, and Troy had managed to gather the courage to bring up the subject he had come to talk about.

"So," he said nervously, "here's the thing. Your freshman honors program at Stanford . . ."

"How'd you hear about that?" Gabriella interrupted.

"A lot of people heard about it," Troy said quietly. "But I wasn't one of them. Why?"

"Because I knew what you would say!" she exclaimed defensively.

"Of course you should do the honors program," he told her. He couldn't believe that she would actually consider *not* going.

Gabriella looked down. "I've been thinking about trying to talk my mom into letting me stay in Albuquerque another year. Take some classes here, go to Stanford when I'm ready," she admitted.

Troy looked at her in shock. "You can't just put off something as amazing as Stanford!" he cried.

Gabriella sighed with exasperation. "So maybe I get to be a little crazy," she admitted. "Everything about my life has been full-speed ahead. This is the first time I've ever even wanted it all to slow down . . . to a stop."

"We're going to graduate," he pointed out. "That's going to happen." Whether we want to or not, he thought.

"Does everything feel that easy for you?" Gabriella asked. "Lucky you, I guess. I get it, it's senior year. This is what happens. But you know what, Troy, my heart doesn't know it's in high school."

That stopped him. He gave her a searching look. Troy started to say something, but Gabriella interrupted him. "Don't say anything else. I'm way better at good-byes than you." She smiled faintly. "I've had a lot of practice."

She kissed him on the cheek and stood up to go inside.

"Wait," Troy said. One word had jumped out at him. "Why are you saying 'good-bye'? You'll be back for prom and graduation."

She hesitated, then said, "I meant good night."

* * *

Back inside her bedroom, Gabriella finally let the tears fall. She knew it was right to attend the honors program and prepare to leave East High behind—but she couldn't help thinking of all the fun she had had and the friends she had made since arriving in Albuquerque.

And Troy . . .

Moments of their time flashed through her mind. Their first meeting at the New Year's Eve party, doing karaoke and finding an unknown side of themselves . . . performing in *Twinkle Towne* . . . working together over the summer at the country club . . . having fun with their friends in the talent show . . .

Gradually, the memories seemed to fade and drift away. That was the past.

She sighed and began to pack some boxes. Like it or not, she was headed into the future.

As soon as Gabriella left for Stanford, East High seemed to become a totally different place.

Troy knew she had made the right decision, but that didn't help when he sat in the rooftop garden . . . alone.

Gabriella's friends were proud of her, but they still missed her when they ate lunch in the cafeteria and noticed her empty seat. Even homeroom wasn't the same without Gabriella.

But perhaps her absence was felt most in the theater. Rehearsals for the spring musical continued, of course, but Troy's heart wasn't really in it. Neither was Kelsi's. Or Taylor's. Or Chad's.

Ms. Darbus could tell that some of the students were dismayed, but they still had a production to rehearse.

"With Miss Montez unavailable to us, the show must go on," Ms. Darbus said firmly. "Sharpay, you'll do Gabriella's duet with Troy. Tiara, are you ready to step in for Sharpay?"

Tiara beamed but tried to look modest. "Those shoes are impossible to fill, Ms. Darbus."

Sharpay gave Tiara a gracious nod of appreci-
ation. "Kelsi will work with you," she told Tiara.
"All right, let's get going. Where's Troy?"

Everyone looked around.

But Troy was nowhere to be found.

In fact, Troy was nowhere in the building. He
was home, missing Gabriella. He went into the
kitchen for a snack and heard a basketball
bouncing in the backyard. He headed outside
and found his dad shooting hoops.

His dad tossed him the ball. Troy caught it and
then sunk a basket.

"How's the big show going?" his father asked,
catching the ball as it bounced on the concrete.

Troy sighed. "You don't want to know."

His dad spun around and tried for a basket.
He missed. Troy grabbed the rebound and
started maneuvering for his own shot.

"If I'm honest, I'm glad you're getting tired of
it," his dad admitted. "I mean, when did you
plan to tell me about this Juilliard thing?"

"Nothing to tell," Troy said, trying to sound casual, just before he launched the ball in the air.

This time he missed the shot. His dad caught the ball and stood still.

"Well, maybe there is," he said slowly. "I'm hearing you're thinking about other schools."

Troy glanced at his dad uncomfortably. "U of A isn't the only school that's talked to me, Dad. You know that."

"But it's the only school *we've* talked about," Mr. Bolton said. "Hey, Chad would be pretty disappointed if you changed your mind, for one thing."

"He'd get over it," Troy replied. "Would you?" he asked.

His dad sighed. "We've been going to U of A games ever since you were a little kid. All you ever talked about is being in a Redhawk uniform."

Troy nodded, but he had to finally be honest with his father. "Only thing is, I'm not a little kid anymore. You raised me to make my own choices. I'm the one who needs to make them, not you or Chad or anyone else."

Troy turned and headed toward the house.

"Hey, Troy . . ." his dad called out.

But Troy didn't turn around. Coach Bolton walked inside, just in time to see Troy heading out the front door and getting into his truck. Coach Bolton started to follow, but his wife reached out a hand to stop him, an under-standing expression on her face.

Troy was trying to figure out where he was going next—and his parents were trying to figure out how to let him go.

Troy knew exactly what would make him feel more at ease. He headed to East High and used his "secret key" to open the door to the Wildcats' locker room. He glanced over at his locker and continued walking down the Hall of Champions. He headed toward the theater and got up on the stage, the place where he and Gabriella had learned something important about themselves and each other. He thought about what next year would be like, without his friends, his team, and Gabriella, and suddenly he felt like screaming.

Instead, he sang a song he'd been learning for the musical, a song that expressed all the confusion and heartache he was feeling.

From the darkness came the sound of one person clapping.

Troy looked up, startled to see Ms. Darbus coming down the aisle.

"Um . . . I know I'm not supposed to be here, Ms. Darbus . . ." he began.

The drama teacher looked at him curiously. "Nor am I, but I'm trying to rebalance a show in which Sharpay is now playing Miss Montez." She gave him a shrewd, questioning look. "And the reason for your visit is . . . ?"

He hesitated. "I guess I feel like this is a really good place to—" He stopped, embarrassed.

"Scream?" she suggested. "Feel free."

"Or just to think," he said.

She nodded. "The stage is a wonderful partner

in the process of self-discovery," she said. "You seem very comfortable up there."

"I do?" Troy asked, surprised.

"Yes," she replied with conviction. "Which is why I submitted an application in your name to Juilliard."

"It was you?" he asked, sounding even more surprised.

"Better to consider these opportunities now, than in ten years when life might limit your choices," she said, her voice softening a bit. "If I've overstepped, I apologize."

He shook his head. "I'm not mad . . . just confused."

"What I've learned from the stage is to trust one's instincts," she said. "And that takes courage, a quality you don't seem to lack." As she walked away, she added, "Stay as long as you like. Last one out turns off the lights."

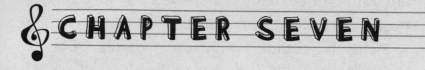

CHAPTER SEVEN

Gradually, Gabriella got used to being at Stanford. At first it was a little scary—all those new people, new professors, and a dorm room. But it was also really cool. As she walked to her first class, she spotted a sign that said WELCOME FRESHMAN HONORS CLASS—and it was printed in five languages! She grinned and felt a small thrill of excitement. It *was* amazing to be here, at the university she had dreamed about attending for so many years, and to be meeting people from all over the world.

Still, she couldn't help but wonder what her old friends were doing back at East High. . . .

The East High auditorium was buzzing with activity, just as it had before every other big show. Unfortunately, not all of the activity was going particularly well.

In fact, almost none of it was.

Troy and Chad were snapping at each other. Sharpay was bossing Ryan around even more than usual. And Zeke and Jason just goofed off the entire time, until finally they actually knocked down an entire set!

The musical was falling apart in front of everyone's eyes. And no one was more dismayed than Kelsi, who was watching the disaster unfold with an impending sense of doom. She sat slumped on her piano bench, her head in her hands, when Troy approached her.

"Hey, I'm sorry I've been messing up your songs a little," he said.

She brushed his apology aside. "It's all of us!" she cried. "And all of us pretty much know why. If it wasn't for Gabriella, our last musical would just be the Sharpay show."

He nodded as he thought that over. He knew exactly what she meant.

That same day, Gabriella was standing in the university quad near a fountain, taking in the college scene around her.

She saw students rushing to class, lying on the grass reading and exchanging hellos.

She saw friends walking together, talking and laughing.

She saw couples walking hand in hand.

She took it all in, deep in thoughts of her own.

A few days later, Troy and Chad walked into the Boltons' kitchen after picking up Troy's tuxedo

93

at the rental shop. Troy showed it to his mom, who looked impressed.

"Wow, gorgeous!" she exclaimed.

"I'd like to take credit, but Gabriella picked it out," Troy said.

"And I've ordered a corsage that's going to perfectly match her dress," his mom said with a smile.

Just then, Troy's cell phone rang. He looked at his phone and saw Gabriella's picture. He smiled. It's almost like we have ESP, he thought as he answered.

When he listened to what Gabriella had to say, however, his smile gradually disappeared. "Don't even say that!" he argued, trying to stop what he was hearing. He headed toward his bedroom.

"Gabriella, the prom is in two days," he protested. "You're supposed to be on an airplane."

She sighed. "It's taken me two weeks to get used to being away from you, from East High, and from all my friends," she said, doing her best to make him understand.

Chad was worried as he stood in the hallway and listened to Troy's conversation. He didn't need to hear what Gabriella was saying to know this phone call wasn't going well.

But Troy wasn't aware of Chad standing there. He took a deep breath and continued to listen.

"So I come back and go to the prom and I leave again? And then it's graduation, and I leave again?" Gabriella's voice trembled. "I don't think I can do it. I think I've run out of good-byes, Troy. I really have. I need to stay right where I am. I'm sorry."

She hung up the phone in tears.

Troy stared at the now silent phone, stunned. "She's not coming back," he said quietly.

"What?" Chad was shocked. "And miss prom?"

Troy nodded.

"Whoa," Chad replied. "Hey, that's lousy, man. It really is."

Chad could tell this wasn't helping much. He

tried to think of something that would cheer up Troy, get his mind off his troubles . . .

And just like that, he knew exactly the right words to say. "School ends, and you don't take the girl with you, right? Gabriella is one step ahead, as usual." He gave Troy a meaningful look. "But now, you snap out of it, dude. We're all starting over. She's at Stanford, Taylor's heading to Yale. We're at U of A. Whole new ball game."

That should do it, Chad thought, satisfied. It was as good a pep talk as any he had ever given the Wildcats, and those had always worked.

Troy looked at Chad in frustration. "Maybe I don't see my life as a 'ball game' anymore, okay?"

The two friends stared at each other, each of them unsure about what to say next.

Troy thought about what Chad had just said. Maybe this time, he thought, he would be one step ahead of Gabriella. And then he knew exactly what he had to do.

CHAPTER EIGHT

Two days later, dusk was beginning to fall as the Wildcats started arriving at East High for the prom. The gym had been transformed with lights and decorations into a fantasyland. Chad and Taylor walked through the entrance, smiling and looking around in disbelief at the gym where so many hard-fought basketball games had been played. They were closely followed by Sharpay and Zeke, Ryan and Kelsi, and Martha and Jason. But two particular people were quite obviously missing. . . .

Back at Stanford, Gabriella was sitting alone in a classroom, finishing a very long equation on the chalkboard and trying to not think about the prom. She knew that it was about time for it to start. Her friends were probably arriving at the gym right now, dressed in their prom finery. Fortunately, she had this extremely complicated math problem to focus on, which helped to keep her thoughts off the dance and all the fun she was missing. . . .

And then she solved the equation.

She stood still for a moment, looking at the board. Sighing, she picked up her book bag and headed out into the golden late-afternoon sunlight.

This late in the day, the quad was almost deserted. As Gabriella walked toward her dorm, she glanced over at the parking area and did a double take. For a moment, she thought she spotted Troy's truck there. But how could that be, when Troy was back in Albuquerque? Maybe, she thought, she just missed him so much that she was seeing things. . . .

"Figured you'd be the last one out of the building," a voice said from behind her.

She whirled around. Now she was *sure* that she was hearing things because that voice sounded exactly like Troy's.

Something made her look up into the branches of a nearby tree—and there he was, wearing a tuxedo and basketball shoes. He grinned down at her.

"I don't believe this!" She gasped.

"I took a wrong turn on the way to my prom," he said. "And so did you."

She started to smile. "You're so crazy. What is it about you and trees?"

He shrugged. "I see things clearly from up here."

"You look handsome," she said, taking in his elegant attire. "But prom is . . . tonight. In

Albuquerque. And that's a thousand miles away."

He shook his head. "My prom is wherever you are," he said in a serious tone. He tossed her a corsage. "And if I'm going to have a last dance at East High, it's going to be with you."

Gabriella hesitated slightly, then held out her hand. Troy jumped down from the tree and took her in his arms.

They began dancing around the quad, just as they had when they were learning to waltz together in the school's rooftop garden. Troy twirled Gabriella out, and when she twirled back, she felt as if she was actually wearing her prom dress. She gazed into Troy's eyes and smiled.

As they continued to dance around the quad under a giant tree at their own private prom, their friends were dancing, too. The other Wildcats swept across the gym floor in each others' arms and somehow, they all felt that Troy and Gabriella were there with them.

* * *

The sun was setting by the time Troy and Gabriella had finished dancing. They strolled around the quad, enjoying the last light of the day.

"It's the best prom I could have imagined, Troy," Gabriella said dreamily.

"Well, if I learned to waltz, it's all your fault," Troy joked.

He then looked at Gabriella seriously. "But it's not just me who changed when you came to East High," he continued. "Kids I used to just pass in the hallway, now we're all friends. And we're all supposed to do a show together. East High changed when you got there, and now it's changed because you left."

Troy took a step back and looked into Gabriella's eyes. "You may be ready to say good-bye to East High, but East High isn't ready to say good-bye to you."

CHAPTER NINE

The sign in front of the theater at East High read: TONIGHT—A HIGH SCHOOL MUSICAL—SENIOR YEAR.

A buzz of anticipation filled the auditorium as the audience members took their seats. But behind the scenes there was a different kind of buzz—the buzz of total chaos! The cast was warming up and trying to settle their nerves, the tech crew was making last-minute checks of the sound and lights, and the costume department was trying to make sure everyone's clothes looked just right.

Sharpay swept grandly through all of the confusion, heading for her dressing room. Suddenly, Jimmie popped out in front of her from behind a curtain.

"We haven't formally met, even though I feel we know each other on a . . . sort of vibey level," he said confidently. "I'm Jimmie 'the Rocket' Zara. And—"

"'Jimmie *the Rocket*'?" Sharpay asked in disbelief. "What are you, some sort of Muppet gangster?"

She suddenly caught a whiff of his cologne. And it did *not* smell good. She sneezed violently.

"Is that your cologne or a toxic spill?" she snipped.

"I bought it for the show," he explained eagerly. "It's called Babe Magnet."

Sharpay rolled her eyes. "Get out of my way!"

she huffed. She turned to the stage manager. "Send Troy in to see me; we need to run the song."

She shoved Jimmie aside and stomped away just as his cell phone beeped.

He pulled it out of his pocket. His face lit up when he saw who was sending the text message.

"Hey, it's Troy," Jimmie said to Donny, who was standing next to him. And then, just to make sure Donny got the point—*Troy Bolton was contacting Jimmie!*—he added, "Troy Bolton is sending me a text. Checking in."

Then he read the text out loud. " 'Been driving all night. I'll try and get there for the second act. Break a leg.' " He looked at Donny, puzzled. " 'Break a leg?' I don't get it."

Donny grinned at him. "Dude, I think it's showbiz for 'you're going on.' "

Jimmie's face turned pale. "As *Troy*?" he asked, hoping that he had misunderstood. "On*stage*?"

"That *so* rocks!" Donny exclaimed. He sounded genuinely excited for his friend.

Of course Donny sounds psyched, Jimmie thought. *He* isn't the guy doomed to make a fool of himself in front of the cast and crew, and a packed auditorium! Jimmie would never live this down, *never*. And his high school career had been going *so well* up until now. . . .

Fortunately, Jimmie's bleak thoughts were interrupted by Ms. Darbus, who rushed up to them and asked, "No Troy?"

When they shook their heads, she said to Donny, "Get word to Kelsi." She turned to Jimmie, who looked as if he were frozen in place.

"Ms. Darbus, I think he stopped breathing!" Donny exclaimed.

She looked around for help. "Get him oxygen!" she yelled. "It's showtime!"

Kelsi was standing in the orchestra pit, ready to bring down her baton to start the overture.

Just as the lights dimmed, Donny jumped into the pit and whispered something in her ear.

For just a second, her eyes widened with alarm. Then she took a deep breath. Whatever happened tonight, happened. This musical was about to begin, and nothing could stop it.

She brought down her baton. The music swelled and *Senior Year* began! A whistle blew loudly. Cheerleaders charged onto the stage to join Wildcats basketball players for the big "championship game" scene. Chad took center stage as the Wildcats won—again!

The audience's cheering was as enthusiastic as it had been at the actual championship game. Chad grinned and realized that being onstage performing in a musical wasn't so goofy after all. Without thinking, he turned to catch Troy's eye—and then he remembered. Troy wasn't there. A little deflated, Chad exited to the wings.

As the singing and dancing continued

onstage, Sharpay was in her dressing room putting the finishing touches on her makeup. Once she was satisfied that her lip gloss was absolutely perfect, she hung out backstage to watch Ryan finish his big song, "I Want It All," surrounded by dancers doing high kicks.

He did a good job, Sharpay thought, as applause filled the room. Quite respectable, in fact. But now, *now* it was finally *her* chance! And she was going to show everyone how a *real* star performed!

She swept through the French doors that led to the balcony set. The audience clapped and cheered for her dramatic entrance. She began singing "Just Want to Be with You," and turned to where Troy should have been standing to join her in their duet.

But Troy was still nowhere to be found.

Sharpay looked around anxiously, a noticeable frown on her face.

Missing a cue during a live performance was

an unpardonable mistake! Not *only* did it disrupt the play, but it made *her* look bad! She would certainly have something to say to Troy as soon as this scene was over!

Her angry thoughts were interrupted by a sudden noise behind her. Jimmie, dressed in a combination of Wildcats' basketball gear and fancy clothes, had stumbled onto the balcony. Sharpay whirled around.

Then Jimmie, his eyes wide with panic, started singing. And it was clear from the first note that he was not a good singer.

Sharpay was livid. Her mind raced as she tried to figure out how she could possibly save this scene, this play, and, in fact, her whole career— but before she could come up with a plan of action, there was another disaster.

She started sneezing.

And it wasn't just one little sneeze, the kind that could easily be covered up. It was a full-blown, serial sneeze attack!

The audience roared. Her eyes watering,

Sharpay stalked off the stage, just in time to see Troy and Gabriella burst through the back door.

Troy was dressed in his jeans and tuxedo jacket; Gabriella was wearing her Stanford sweater. They headed straight for the stage, passing Sharpay, who was still sneezing and coughing and trying to make her way to her dressing room.

"Perfect," she snapped as they ran past her. *Of course* Troy and Gabriella were here to save the day—and steal her spotlight. Why shouldn't history repeat itself? "Go for it. Save the day. Whoopee," she said with defeat.

As she walked wearily to her dressing room, Troy and Gabriella ran toward the stage. Troy jumped down to the orchestra pit to climb the tree to the balcony where Gabriella would be waiting.

Their sudden appearance surprised everyone— and lifted everyone's spirits, too. Gabriella and Troy began singing "Just Want to Be with You."

The entire cast was smiling. Suddenly, the show was fantastic!

When Sharpay finally made it to her dressing room, she discovered Tiara sitting in front of her makeup mirror, wearing one of her dresses.

Sharpay's mouth dropped open. It took her several seconds to understand what she was seeing. Then she yelled, "That's my dress!"

Tiara nodded calmly. "Had one made just like it. Only better." She smiled at Sharpay in the mirror. "I'm playing Sharpay, remember? Do you mind stepping aside? I need to warm up and give a good first impression, since it will be *my* drama department next year."

Sharpay's mind was reeling. What was happening here? Where had the meek, unassuming, hero-worshipping Tiara gone? And who was this upstart in her place?

"You're not a singer, you're a London school-girl!" Sharpay protested.

Tiara smiled smugly. "Yes . . . London Academy

of Dramatic Arts. I took the job with you to learn the theater ropes at East High. Now I have."

"But you were so . . . humble!" Sharpay insisted.

"That's called acting," Tiara replied. "You should try it some time."

Then she swept out of the room and onto the stage for her scene.

Tiara began to sing "A Night to Remember" in her role as Sharpay. Listening from the dressing room, Sharpay had to admit that Tiara sounded good. *Really* good.

Life was so terribly unfair.

She put her head down on the dressing table and sighed. She had been defeated, and she knew it. Sharpay could hear the audience cheering—not for her, but for the person who was playing her!

Life was *despicably* unfair.

Then, deep inside of Sharpay, her fighting instinct began to kick in.

She lifted her head. So what if life wasn't

always picture-perfect? She was Sharpay Evans—and no little pip-squeak imitator could take that away from her!

She began shadowboxing in the mirror to psych herself up. Then she said to her reflection, "If East High is going to remember one Sharpay . . . it's going to be *me!*"

She noted with approval that her reflection looked determined, purposeful, and powerful. In other words, like the *real* Sharpay Evans. She ran to her clothes rack and began sifting through her wardrobe. She had to find the perfect outfit and she had to find it *now.*

Tiara was still onstage, still singing, still basking in the limelight—when suddenly the crowd gasped.

Sharpay was being lowered to the stage from the rafters, dressed in the same dress Tiara was wearing, only with more bling, more flounce, more star presence. She landed right in front of her new rival and began to sing.

And then East High was treated to a singing showdown that would be remembered for years to come! It was Sharpay versus Tiara, two super-star divas who both loved the spotlight—and neither would give an inch. As they sang a dueling version of "A Night to Remember," the rest of the cast and crew watched in awe.

It was a showstopper to end all showstoppers, and when it was over, the curtain fell. *Senior Year* was a smashing success.

CHAPTER TEN

The curtain rose again, revealing the cast wearing their caps and gowns.

"Ladies and gentlemen," Ms. Darbus announced, "our seniors."

As she read their names, each student took his or her turn in the spotlight.

"Martha Cox," Ms. Darbus said. "University of Southern California. Dance."

Martha bowed, grinning from ear to ear.

"Zeke Baylor," Ms. Darbus continued. "Teen Chef of the Year, Cornell University. Culinary."

He bowed with a flourish.

"Kelsi Nielsen. The Juilliard School. Music."

Kelsi froze in the spotlight before taking her bow, shock written all over her face. She couldn't believe she won the Juilliard scholarship.

"Jason Cross." As Jason moved into the spotlight, she added dryly, "You did it. You graduated."

Jason cast his eyes to the ceiling in thanks and then moved to the side.

"Taylor McKessie," Ms. Darbus called out. "Yale University. Magna Cum Laude. Political Science."

Taylor tried to play it cool, but she couldn't help showing how excited she was.

As Sharpay and Ryan stood next to each other, waiting their turn, Ms. Darbus glanced at the note in her hand.

"I'm pleased to announce that due to the excellence displayed here this evening, Juilliard has made an extraordinary decision," she said.

"Another senior is now offered a Juilliard scholarship . . ."

As everyone in the audience seemed to turn their attention toward Sharpay, she broke out into a huge smile.

Ms. Darbus knew how to create drama. She paused for just a moment before saying, "Congratulations, Mr. Ryan Evans. Choreography."

Stunned, Ryan glanced nervously at his sister. He didn't know how Sharpay was going to handle the news.

But Sharpay pushed him gently toward the center of the stage and then led the applause.

As Sharpay stood onstage, smiling at her brother, Ms. Darbus added, "And as I will be taking a sabbatical next fall, I can now reveal with great pride my choice to run East High's Drama Department during my absence." She turned and gestured to Sharpay. "Congratulations and thank you . . . Miss Sharpay Evans."

As surprised applause rippled through the theater, Sharpay winked at Ryan. She stepped forward to take her bow and turned to wave to Tiara, who was standing backstage with a dismayed expression on her face. Finally, Sharpay waved to her mom, then stepped back into the line.

Ms. Darbus waited until the audience had quieted down, then said, "And now, a senior who, I believe, has a decision to make. Mr. Troy Bolton. Troy?"

The spotlight hit Troy. "And I've chosen basketball," he announced.

Behind him, his friends all nodded. They had been expecting this.

"But I've also chosen theater," he revealed.

Eyebrows were raised as everyone wondered what this meant.

"The University of California in Berkeley offers me both," he said. "And that's where I'll be going next fall."

Now everyone was whispering to each other about this sudden twist. Everyone except Chad, that is, who looked totally shocked.

Troy reached for Gabriella's hand and gazed into her eyes. "Most of all, I choose the person who inspires my heart, which is why I picked a school that's exactly 32.7 miles from . . . you." He pulled her toward him so they could stand in the spotlight together. "Gabriella Montez," he said, making the announcement for Ms. Darbus. "Stanford University. School of Law."

For one long moment, Troy and Gabriella shared a look that seemed as if it might last forever.

Then the audience burst into applause, and Troy stepped back, allowing Gabriella to stand alone at center stage.

"Next, Mr. Chad Danforth, University of Albuquerque," Ms. Darbus said. "Basketball scholarship."

But as the audience cheered for Chad, his friends looked around, only to discover that the spot where he had been standing was now vacant.

"He's gone!" Taylor cried.

Troy didn't have to think twice. He knew exactly where Chad would be.

He took off running.

Sure enough, as Troy burst through the gym doors, he saw Chad on the court, wearing his cap and gown and shooting hoops.

Troy came to a stop and watched. How many hours had he and Chad spent in this gym, practicing, competing, laughing? As excited as Troy was about everything that lay ahead of him, he also felt a twinge of sadness at everything that would now be part of his past.

Chad seemed to be having the same thoughts. He glanced at Troy and said, "So I guess when they hand us the diploma, we're actually done here."

"What makes you think we're getting diplomas?" Troy asked, trying to make a joke.

Chad gave him a faint grin in response. "One question. Does Berkeley play . . ."

"Yep, we're scheduled to kick the Redhawks'

butts next November," Troy responded.

Chad's grin widened. So this wouldn't be the last time he and Troy were on the court together after all!

"Game on, hoops," he said.

They knocked fists—and then Troy stole the ball from Chad and went racing down the court, with his best friend right behind him. Before they knew it, they were laughing and doing their best to beat each other in a game of one-on-one. They had stopped thinking about what the future held, or how their friendship would change, or even what it would feel like to actually graduate.

Just then, a voice boomed through the gym. "Danforth! Bolton!" Coach Bolton yelled. "Get out there and get onstage!"

Troy stopped in his tracks and looked at Chad. "Now there's something I never thought I'd hear my dad say." He grinned.

They ran toward the gym door. As they passed Coach Bolton, he stopped Troy and gave him a proud look. Troy and his dad gave each other a quick hug. Now it was time to get to the stadium and graduate!

The football stadium was filled with parents, sisters, brothers, and friends as the Wildcats prepared for one last big moment at East High: graduation.

The seniors were lined up for their entrance, the buzz of happy laughter and conversation in the stadium was being shushed, and the processional was finally about to begin. This was it.

One by one, the Wildcats marched across the stage to get their diplomas, smiling broadly as their family and friends applauded for them. Suddenly, Troy stepped up to the podium to make an official address.

"East High is a place where teachers encouraged us to break the status quo and define ourselves as we choose." He glanced over at Ms. Darbus. "Where a jock can cook up a mean crème brûlée, and a brainiac can break it down on the dance floor. It's a place where one person, if it's the right person—" He looked over at Gabriella. "—changes us all."

Troy cleared his throat and looked around at all his friends, the people he had gone to school with and had fun with and learned from. The people he would never forget.

"East High is having friends we'll keep for the rest of our lives. And that means we really *are*—" He grinned at the senior class. "—all in this together. Once a Wildcat, *always* a Wildcat!"

Cheering, everyone threw their caps into the air and ran across the football field in celebration. The high spirits were contagious, and soon the senior class was singing and dancing, almost as if they couldn't leave East High without one last song. But as they reached the end of the field, the Wildcats turned around for one more look at the place that had changed their lives. After all, this was the end of high school—the end of four years of friendship and fun and of discoveries and changes that they couldn't have imagined on that first day at East High, which seemed like it was so long ago. They couldn't help wishing that, in some way, high school wouldn't end.

And then the Wildcats exited their stage for the very last time, on the way to meet their futures.

EPILOGUE

Jimmie, Donny, and some other new members of the Wildcats bounded into the Wildcats locker room. It was the off-season, of course, and there wasn't a basketball practice scheduled, but they couldn't wait to get on the court and shoot some hoops.

They each opened up their lockers and found a basketball inside, with a combination written on it.

They turned at the same time to look at the

lockers that Troy Bolton and Chad Danforth had used all during their high school careers as Wildcats.

Now Jimmie's and Donny's names were on the lockers, written on tape and stuck over Troy's and Chad's.

The two sophomores opened their new lockers and, with a little shiver of awe, discovered that each one held a pair of the rattiest, smelliest gym socks on the planet.

"They left us their lucky socks!" Jimmie exclaimed.

"Still haven't been washed," Donny whispered.

"Wow!" Jimmie was grinning from ear to ear. "Those dudes are so cool."

He and Donny looked at each other. Without asking, they knew they each had the same thought.

"What team?" Donny yelled.

"Wildcats!!!" Jimmie responded.

"What team?" Donny said again.

"Wildcats!" Jimmie responded.

"What team?" Donny shouted one last time.

"Wildcats!" Jimmie and the other players yelled. "Getcha head in the game!"

Everyone gave each other high fives. They couldn't wait for the new school year to begin.